Late for the Library!

by Peter Maloney
and Felicia Zekauskas

SCHOLASTIC INC.
New York   Toronto   London   Auckland   Sydney
Mexico City   New Delhi   Hong Kong   Buenos Aires

To Kristin Maloney, Cathy Thompson,
and the more than 136,000 other librarians
in the United States today.

ISBN 0-439-55361-X

12 11 10 9 8 7 6 5 4 3 2 1   4 5 6 7 8 9/0

Printed in the U.S.A.
First printing, January 2004

Chapter 1
Favorite Books

One day, Mrs. Robinson asked everybody in the class to bring in a favorite book.

Tobi brought in a book about bats.

Felicia brought in a book about a girl who saves the day . . . with her hair bow!

Rich brought in a book about a boy
who dreams of doing something really
important!
And Peter brought in a book about
a magic hockey stick.

"Each day, I'll read one book to the class until I've read every one," said Mrs. Robinson.

CHAPTER 2
A Long Wait

Peter couldn't wait for Mrs. Robinson
to read his book.

But Peter had to wait.
It was almost two weeks before
Mrs. Robinson finally read his book.

"That was a wonderful story," said
Mrs. Robinson when she finished.
"Can you tell us anything about
the book?"

"Like what?" asked Peter.

"Maybe how long you've had it or where you got it," said Mrs. Robinson.

"I got it when we were on summer vacation over a year ago," said Peter.

"And where did you get it?" asked
Mrs. Robinson.

"I got it out of the . . . " Peter stopped.
A terrible thought suddenly occurred
to him.
"I mean, I got it as a . . . a . . . uh . . .
gift!" said Peter.

CHAPTER 3
Long Overdue

Peter suddenly had remembered where his book came from.
A public library!
Peter knew if a library book is returned late there is a late fee . . . sometimes up to 25 cents a day!

Peter remembered going to the
library with his parents.
But he couldn't remember if he had
checked out any books.
It had been so long ago—more than
365 days!

Later that day, Peter asked Felicia,
"What does 365 times 25 equal?"
Felicia was good at math.

"A lot!" said Felicia.

"Could you be more exact?"
asked Peter.

"An awful lot!" said Felicia.

CHAPTER 4
Library Day

The next day, Mrs. Robinson's class visited the school library.

"I have a question," Peter said very softly to Ms. Lerner, the school librarian.

"I can hardly hear you," said Ms. Lerner.

"I thought we were supposed to whisper in the library," said Peter.

"That is true," said Ms. Lerner. "But whisper just a little bit louder."

"Well," said Peter. "I . . . I mean, a friend of mine . . . has a problem. He has a library book that he never returned."

"Oh!" said Ms. Lerner. "That is a problem! How late is your friend's book?"

"Over a year," said Peter.

"Oh, my!" said Ms. Lerner. "At 25 cents a day, that would add up to . . . well . . . an awful lot."

"Exactly!" said Peter. "What do you think my friend should do?"

"Maybe if he would bring in the book, I could help," said Ms. Lerner.

"I have it right here!"
said Peter.

"Do you think
I could borrow
it?" asked
Ms. Lerner.

"Sure," said
Peter. "After all,
this is a library."

21

CHAPTER 5
A Comic Idea

Back in class, Peter stared out the window.
"Is anything the matter?" asked Mrs. Robinson.

"No," said Peter. "I'm fine."
But Peter wasn't fine.
He had to raise an awful lot of money
—in a hurry!

Peter thought . . .

and thought . . .

and thought.

Suddenly, Peter jumped out of his seat.
"I've got it!" he cried.

"Got what?" asked Mrs. Robinson.
Everybody was looking at Peter.

"Nothing," said Peter.

CHAPTER 6
Ms. Lerner Lends a Hand

The next morning on the playground,
Felicia called to Peter.
"Did you see this?" she asked.
"Someone is selling their comic books.
And they sound just like yours!"

"They are mine," said Peter. "I'm selling them."

"But why?" asked Felicia. "You love your comics."
Just then, the school bell rang.

Ms. Lerner stopped Peter in the hallway.
"I called the library," said Ms. Lerner.
"And I have some good news for your friend."

"What is it?" asked Peter.

"The book isn't overdue at all," said Ms. Lerner.

"It has to be!" said Peter. "My friend has had it since last summer."

"It's not overdue," said Ms. Lerner.
"The book wasn't borrowed.
It was bought—at a library book sale!"

"So I can keep it?" asked Peter.

"Of course you can't," said Ms. Lerner.

"But your friend can!"